W9-DBA-236

STRONG, HEALTHY GIRLS

DEALING WITH DRAMA

By Lauren Emily Whalen

CONTENT CONSULTANT

Dr. Amanda J. Rose
Professor of Psychological Sciences
University of Missouri

An Imprint of Abdo Publishing | abdobooks.com

abdobooks.com

Published by Abdo Publishing, a division of ABDO, PO Box 398166, Minneapolis, Minnesota 55439.

Printed in the United States of America, North Mankato, Minnesota.
082020
012021

Cover Photo: iStockphoto
Interior Photos: Wunder Visuals/iStockphoto, 8, 56; iStockphoto, 11, 22, 32, 34, 42, 48, 54, 59, 68; Shutterstock Images, 12, 38–39, 50–51, 87; Katarzyna Bialasiewicz/iStockphoto, 15; SDI Productions/iStockphoto, 16; AJ Watt/iStockphoto, 20; People Images/iStockphoto, 24, 73; Light Field Studios/iStockphoto, 26; Nicolas McComber/iStockphoto, 30; Antonio Diaz/Shutterstock Images, 37; Svitlana Sokolova/Shutterstock Images, 44; Antonio Diaz/iStockphoto, 47, 93; Wave Break Media/Shutterstock Images, 62, 98; Antonio Guillem/Shutterstock Images, 65; Monkey Business Images/iStockphoto, 70; Pete Karici/iStockphoto, 74; Borysevych.com/Shutterstock Images, 80; Antonio Guillem/iStockphoto, 82; Bojan Milinkov/Shutterstock Images, 84; Ghislain & Marie David de Lossy/iStockphoto, 90; Prostock Studio/iStockphoto, 94; Wave Break Media/iStockphoto, 97

Editor: Aubrey Zalewski
Series Designer: Nikki Nordby

Library of Congress Control Number: 2019954413
Publisher's Cataloging-in-Publication Data

Names: Whalen, Lauren Emily, author.
Title: Dealing with drama / by Lauren Emily Whalen
Description: Minneapolis, Minnesota : Abdo Publishing, 2021 | Series: Strong, healthy girls | Includes online resources and index.
Identifiers: ISBN 9781532192159 (lib. bdg.) | ISBN 9781098210052 (ebook)
Subjects: LCSH: Interpersonal conflict in adolescence--Juvenile literature. | Stress in youth--Juvenile literature. | Coping behavior--Juvenile literature. | Attitude (Psychology)--Juvenile literature. | Sociology of friendship--Juvenile literature. | Mean girls--Juvenile literature.
Classification: DDC 155.533--dc23

CONTENTS

DR. AMANDA

Dr. Amanda J. Rose has always been interested in relationships. Our closest relationships can bring us incredible happiness, but when our relationships don't go well, life can be very hard. Different relationships are especially important at different stages of life, with friendships being especially important for adolescents. Dr. Amanda has been studying girls' friendships for over 20 years, with more than 5,000 youth participating in her research projects.

Dr. Amanda grew up in Ohio and went to college at the Ohio State University. There, she majored in psychology and minored in English. Her senior thesis was her first research project on adolescence. After graduating summa cum laude, Dr. Amanda went on to study developmental psychology at the University of Illinois at Urbana-Champaign. There, she earned her master's degree and her doctorate. For her master's thesis and doctoral dissertation, she studied how girls and boys handle conflict in their friendships and how they support each other in times of stress.

In 1999, Dr. Amanda joined the faculty at the University of Missouri as a founding member of the Developmental Psychology Training Program in the Department of Psychological Sciences. Together with her students, she has conducted many research studies, with a focus on the benefits and challenges of girls' friendships. This research has been funded by the National Institute of Mental Health. During her time at the University of Missouri, Dr. Amanda has received many honors and awards, including an Early Scientific Achievement Award from the Society for Research in Child Development and a Kemper Fellowship for Excellence in Teaching, one of the highest teaching honors awarded at the University of Missouri.

Dr. Amanda lives in Columbia, Missouri, with her husband, her teenage daughter and son, and her yellow Labrador retriever, Charlie.

TAKE IT FROM ME

When I was a teen, I prided myself on not getting involved in other people's drama or creating my own. Looking back, I realize how much I actually did both. I wasn't a gossip, but I was the designated listener in my group of friends. So at any given time, I knew exactly who was mad at whom or who was on the verge of breaking up with her boyfriend.

As for my own drama, I made plenty of it. I cried when I didn't get straight As. I agonized over every word my boyfriend said. Before I started dating, I often openly wondered what was "wrong" with me. Drama central. As for dealing with drama, let's just say a *lot* of locker doors were slammed, and the occasional rumor was spread.

A lot of changes happen when you enter high school. Often you're meeting a lot of new people and developing different interests. Your homework load might amp up as well, leading you to spend more time studying. A different environment can be great for making friends but can also lead to drama.

It's easy to say, "I don't do drama"—you may have told yourself and others this very thing in the past. After all, who wants to have conflicts with friends or tension with classmates? But in reality, drama is a lot more complicated. Even when you have a great group of friends, drama can arise within your circle. There's friend-on-friend teasing and conflicts along with incompatible behaviors and goals. How can you tell when a friend's "I'm just kidding" has gone too far? How do you know when conflicts become deal breakers? And when a friend's behavior goes full-on mean girl, what do you do?

At this point you might be asking yourself, "How do I avoid *any* drama?" Unless you seal yourself in a cave for all of middle school and high school (and where's the fun in that?), you probably can't avoid drama. Conflict is normal and healthy, and this book will give you the tools to resolve it and emerge a better friend and a stronger person!

XOXO,
LAUREN

CHAPTER ONE

TAKING A BREAK

BFF is a term you see everywhere, from hashtags online to heart-shaped necklaces you're supposed to share with your one and only. But many times, best friends *aren't* forever. As you grow older and your interests and priorities change, it's normal to gravitate toward new people who share your thoughts and passions—and sometimes old friends get left behind.

Drifting apart from childhood BFFs is natural, but that doesn't make it hurt any less, especially when you're the one trying to keep the friendship together. What happens when formerly tight-knit friendships start to loosen? When Carmen and her best friend, Shane, started high school, they found themselves drifting apart as Carmen never thought they would.

CARMEN'S STORY

Carmen and Shane met in pre-K and instantly clicked over sharing their favorite purple crayon. From then on, they were best friends. Since the girls played soccer and did community theater together, they were able to see each other all the time and bond over what mattered to them most. Carmen felt unstoppable with Shane by her side. Whether they were acting in plays, scoring goals against the opposing team, or trading purple T-shirts, Carmen knew she had a forever friend. But when Carmen and Shane started high school, things began to change.

"Are you trying out for the soccer team?" Shane asked Carmen the first week of school.

Carmen paused. She knew she'd get to hang out with Shane more if she played soccer, and she thought she was good enough for JV at least. But their high school's team required a lot of practice and training: four practices a week during the season, mandatory workouts all year long, and summer intensives. And though Carmen loved to play, she wasn't sure she wanted to give all her time to soccer.

TALK ABOUT IT

- **Do you have a best friend? How did you meet? What keeps your friendship strong?**
- **What does the phrase *best friends forever* mean to you? Do you think it's possible to stay friends forever?**

Still, Carmen stalled by saying, "I don't know." She then changed the subject. "I saw that the drama club posted auditions for the fall play. Should I sign us up?"

She was surprised to see Shane looking hesitant. "Um," Shane said, looking at Carmen. "I'm not sure I'll have time if I make JV, and . . ." Shane bit her lip. "I think I've outgrown the whole theater thing."

How can you outgrow theater? Carmen thought.

TALK ABOUT IT

- **Have you ever had to choose between two activities you loved? What went into making that decision?**
- **How might friendships change when friends make different life choices?**

After all, most professional actors were adults. Instead of asking Shane straight-out, though—she didn't want to sound possessive or weird—Carmen pasted on a smile. "Well, I'm going to audition. Good luck at soccer tryouts!"

"Good luck to you too," Shane said.

You're supposed to say, "Break a leg," Carmen thought, hiding her disappointment with another forced smile.

***

The next week, Shane made the JV soccer team. Auditions for the fall play weren't for another couple weeks, but Carmen was happy for Shane and made it a point to send purple balloons, which Shane loved, to Shane's house. Even though soccer practice meant the two didn't see each other as often, Carmen tried to keep in touch by sending text messages and making sure to chat with Shane every day after English, the one class they shared.

Slowly but surely, though, Shane started responding to Carmen's texts with one-word answers instead of her usual paragraphs. Pretty soon, Shane stopped replying altogether and even avoided Carmen after English. When audition day arrived, Carmen texted Shane, "I'm so nervous!" Shane didn't reply.

The next day, Carmen found out she'd been cast in a speaking role, which was rare for a freshman. She excitedly texted Shane the news. Still no reply.

Carmen couldn't help it. She burst into tears and stayed in bed all Sunday. What had happened to their friendship? She had known that Shane was busy with soccer, and she had figured that soccer was probably why Shane had stopped responding to texts. But Shane knew how important theater was to Carmen. In the past, Shane had always cheered Carmen on—even when Carmen got bigger roles

Carmen couldn't help it. She burst into tears and stayed in bed all Sunday.

TALK ABOUT IT

- Why do you think Shane stopped replying to Carmen's texts?
- How would you have handled this situation if you were Carmen?
- Do you think face-to-face conversation is better than texting? Why or why not? What are the advantages and disadvantages of each?

She understood that she and Shane were doing different things, but why did their friendship have to stop?

than Shane, which happened more often than not.

Carmen knew that replying to texts or saying hello after class took only a few seconds. Since when was she worth so little to Shane? It's not like she was asking for total devotion. She understood that she and Shane were doing different things, but why did their friendship have to stop? Carmen decided that she needed to talk to Shane face-to-face.

***

On Monday after English, Shane was waiting for Carmen outside the classroom.

"You wanted to talk?" Shane asked. They fell into step as they walked down the hallway, and Carmen felt a tiny bit of hope.

Once they got to her locker, Carmen took a deep breath. She'd thought about what to say, but she wasn't sure how Shane would react. After the past few weeks, she wasn't sure how well she knew her best friend anymore. "I'm just not sure what happened to us," Carmen said, looking down at the textbook still in her hands before she looked back up at Shane.

Shane shrugged, avoiding Carmen's gaze. "I've been busy. You know how soccer is. A lot of practices."

"Right, but . . ." Carmen trailed off. "You used to answer my texts right away. And I was so happy when you made soccer. I thought you'd feel the same way when I got in the play."

"I *am* happy for you!" Shane insisted. "Seriously, we're still friends. I'm just busy."

"You've said that twice now," Carmen pointed out. "Are you too busy for me?" She paused. "I'm not mad, more just . . . sad. I feel like I'm not as important to you anymore."

"I'm not sure what you want me to do about that," Shane said gently. "I can't quit the soccer team. I don't want to." Before Carmen could explain that she didn't want Shane to quit soccer, the bell rang. "I gotta go," Shane told Carmen, already turning to leave. "I'll see you later?"

Carmen tried to smile. "Sure."

TALK ABOUT IT

- **How do you think Shane and Carmen each handled this conversation?**
- **Do you think it's possible for Carmen and Shane to get back the connection they had before?**
- **Have you and a friend ever drifted apart? How did you handle it?**

ASK THE EXPERT

Sadly, when friends grow apart, betrayals become more common. That can mean neglect or outright meanness. Shane wasn't mean, but she became more absorbed in her own interests, and Carmen felt left behind. Shane's words may have been friendly, but her actions showed Carmen that Shane wasn't a good friend anymore.

Friendships are likely to change in adolescence because your environment, interests, body, and mind are in flux. You're shifting as an individual, and it stands to reason that friendships might also shift. Your friendships also become more important to you than they were when you were younger. So the friendships that end now could affect you more at this age than they would have if you were younger.

What can you do when you and a friend drift apart? There are many options. You can let go for the moment and ease back on texting and talking with that friend. You can also write down your feelings.

If you'd like to have a conversation with your friend, that's also OK. Face-to-face is better than over text. Take time to choose your words carefully and be honest about what you're feeling. Talking won't necessarily save the friendship. But even then, you can use that conversation as closure to help you move forward. And no matter what happens, remember that sometimes friends can eventually reconnect.

GET **HEALTHY**

- Know that friendships and people change as they get older.
- If your friend is drifting away, you can let it go and concentrate on other friends. You don't have to confront your friend if you aren't comfortable.
- Try not to text when you're angry. Step back, take deep breaths, and plan what you'll say next.
- Talk in person about difficult things. Be honest about what you're feeling.

THE LAST WORD FROM **LAUREN**

My childhood best friend and I drifted apart when we started high school, and that led to more than one argument. We dealt with it by taking a break and getting more involved in our own activities. For me that was theater, just like Carmen. My friend and I reconnected when we were in college and found new common ground in living away from home for the first time and following our passions. As adults, we live in different states but keep in touch on social media. Sometimes time can heal old wounds, and friends can find one another again years later. What's great about getting older is the possibility of finding new friends and passions—some of which may surprise you. When you begin a new chapter of your life, keep an open mind. Know that not everything will stay the same, but also know that change can be great.

CHAPTER TWO

TIRED OF TEASING

You've found your group of friends—that's great! You share interests, a lunch table, maybe even clothes. What could go wrong? The answer is "a lot."

Friends can push us to be the best version of ourselves, whether that's something as minor as wearing a color you normally wouldn't or as important as becoming more politically active or exploring life's tough questions. But influence from your friends can be negative just as often. What if a friend makes you feel both good and bad? What if someone in your group consistently zeroes in on you in a way that feels negative? And when they claim they're "just kidding," should you push the issue or let it go?

Camila and Eileen were friends as well as basketball teammates. Eileen always had Camila's back on the court—on the sidelines, not so much. Eventually, Camila had to decide whether to laugh off Eileen's hurtful remarks and keep the peace or assert herself and risk alienating her entire friend group.

CAMILA'S STORY

"Why are you wearing *that*?" Eileen asked, giggling, as Camila put her lunch tray down at their usual table. She'd been sitting here every day for the past school year, after meeting Eileen on the varsity basketball team. Eventually, Eileen's friends became Camila's friends. She loved the feeling of belonging that she'd never had in junior high.

Camila looked down at her jeans and *Star Wars* T-shirt, her standard outfit since seventh grade. She had always felt comfortable in casual clothes, and she liked wearing T-shirts that showed off her sci-fi geek side. "Is there a stain or something?"

She loved the feeling of belonging that she'd never had in junior high.

Eileen rolled her eyes. "I just don't get why you dress like a ten-year-old," she said, smoothing down her new top, which was definitely not a *Star Wars* T-shirt.

Camila was surprised at the pang of hurt she felt. She'd always dressed this way—in fact, Eileen had seen this T-shirt before—and this was the first time Eileen had commented on it. Camila looked around at their lunch table, but everyone else was busy unwrapping their food and chatting. Camila looked down at her burrito, unsure what to do.

TALK ABOUT IT

- **What clothes do you like to wear the most? Do you think they capture who you are?**
- **Has a friend ever started teasing you out of the blue? How did that make you feel?**
- **If Camila and Eileen were your friends and you overheard this conversation, what would you do?**

***

The teasing didn't stop there. From then on, Eileen poked fun at Camila's clothes at

least a couple times a week. Usually Eileen waited until none of their other friends were in earshot, and the remarks were never particularly mean. Still, "You're wearing *that*? Again?" wasn't fun for Camila to hear.

Almost more confusing was how great of a friend Eileen was when she wasn't making pointed comments about Camila's wardrobe. She always partnered with Camila for stretches and drills at basketball practice and cheered from the bench when Camila played in games. At sleepovers, she shared her cheese popcorn with Camila first, just like always. Camila wasn't sure what was going on, but every time Eileen made fun of her, Camila just rolled her eyes and hoped ignoring her would help.

But the next time Eileen said, "Are you wearing *that*?" Camila snapped.

"Yes, I am wearing *that*," Camila said in a low whisper, gesturing to her favorite anime shirt. "What's your problem, Eileen?"

Eileen raised her eyebrows and smirked, calmly popping the tab on her soda as the rest of their friends ate. "I'm just kidding. Jeez, lighten up!"

TALK ABOUT IT

- **Why do you think Camila finally reacted to Eileen's teasing about her clothes?**
- **What would you do if one of your friends started making fun of you?**
- **Was Camila taking Eileen's comments too seriously? Why or why not?**
- **Should Camila have kept ignoring Eileen, or should she have done more to shut down the teasing? Why?**

***

Maybe I'm making too big a deal out of this, Camila thought after school that day. She didn't want to confront Eileen about the teasing—after all, Eileen was the one who had introduced Camila to all their friends. And besides, even though they didn't have practice today, the team had an out-of-town basketball tournament coming up. If Camila

Maybe I'm making too big a deal out of this . . .

made an enemy of Eileen, it would be impossible to avoid her on the team bus as well as on the court.

Still, Camila felt she had to do something. She didn't want to change her wardrobe. Eileen was trendier, but Camila was casual, and she liked that about herself. And she worried if she asked Eileen what was going on, Eileen would brush her off and accuse her of overreacting. Again. Anyway, Camila wasn't sure she could

do that without yelling or blowing up at Eileen. And Camila didn't want their friends siding with Eileen over her.

Camila decided to try avoiding Eileen. She could sit at a different lunch table or tell their coach she was sick while she figured out what to do next. But Camila didn't want to ignore her other friends or miss out on the basketball practices she loved. Instead, she partnered with a tall sophomore named Heather for drills at the next practice. At lunch, she started sitting at the other end of the long table with Jen, another girl in the group who shared Camila's crush on Han Solo. When the out-of-town tournament came around, Camila sat next to Heather on the bus. Eileen got on the bus and looked confused. Camila just smiled and looked away.

TALK ABOUT IT

- **Do you think Eileen will keep teasing Camila? Why or why not?**
- **What do you think of Camila's method of dealing with Eileen?**
- **How would you have acted if you were Camila?**

ASK THE

EXPERT

Some friendships are ambivalent, meaning they're both affectionate and annoying. For example, Camila likes the camaraderie she's found with Eileen, the basketball team, and their shared group of friends, but she's understandably not a fan of Eileen's snide remarks about her clothing. Eileen's intent might not be to hurt Camila's feelings. Maybe Eileen is having trouble in her own life, and instead she's taking her frustration out on Camila. But the impact of the teasing on Camila is negative. Even if Eileen thinks she's being friendly, the effect on Camila is just the opposite.

When one person in your friend group is focusing on you in a way that makes you feel uncomfortable, it might be tempting to confront her—but if you do that, you can risk losing even more friends. A good compromise is to maintain a polite distance from the person who's giving you trouble. But if the teasing persists and it's making you uncomfortable, don't be afraid to talk to an adult.

GET HEALTHY

- Teasing can just be friendly—if your pal's jabs don't bother you, don't worry about it.
- If you don't want to confront your friend or cause even more drama, maintain a distance from that friend while still hanging out with your group.
- If you want to confront your friend, keep a calm voice and be direct. Tell her how you feel and ask her to stop. Instead of accusing her, give her the benefit of the doubt. This may help her be less defensive.
- If all you're getting from your friend is negativity, it might be time to start looking for a new friend.

THE LAST WORD FROM LAUREN

My friends and I tease each other all the time! We're close enough to know what's OK to kid about and what's off limits or may require more sensitivity. Once in a while, someone will cross the line, and others will gently but firmly correct her. Knowing when to apologize and change your behavior is a skill that improves with practice and experience.

Teasing can be a way for friends to show love, but when the remarks get hurtful, it's time to act. It's up to you to decide your limits and what actions to take when a friend pushes those limits. Whether you choose to talk to your friend about it, keep your distance, or end things altogether, know that you don't have to decide what to do right away. If you need someone to bounce ideas off of, confide in a parent, teacher, or mentor.

CHAPTER THREE

MISPLACED

It's completely normal to butt heads with your nearest and dearest. After all, we're human, and we're complicated. And we don't always agree or communicate perfectly. This is called conflict. Conflict is normal and healthy but can be tough, especially when you and your friend aren't used to fighting.

Many times, conflict arises from misunderstandings or miscommunications. You know the drill: you say one thing, your friend thinks another, or vice versa. Someone misses a text, and the other person feels like they're being ignored. And if they're not addressed, miscommunications can escalate, resulting in larger conflicts that are much harder to resolve.

Gretchen and Siobhan had a misunderstanding over an item of clothing. On the surface, that's not major. But as the miscommunications continued and the conflict escalated, Siobhan found herself wondering what to do to make things right.

SIOBHAN'S STORY

Friday afternoon, Gretchen met Siobhan at her locker after the final bell rang. "You know that pink top with the scoop neck?"

Gretchen and Siobhan had been close since eighth grade, when Siobhan and her family moved to the United States from Ireland. Even after going from their small junior high to a much larger high school, the girls stayed best friends, sharing several classes and hanging out during the week.

Siobhan nodded, loading up her backpack for the weekend. She felt like she could read Gretchen's mind, and she was pretty sure she knew what Gretchen would ask. "Do you want to borrow it for the dance tomorrow night?" This wasn't an unusual request. Over the years, they had raided each other's bookshelves, music collections, and—since they were the same size—closets.

Gretchen nodded eagerly. "You read my mind, S! Thank you so much. I'll take good care of it."

"I know." Siobhan put her arm around her friend as they made their way down the hall together.

TALK ABOUT IT

- **Why might friends share clothes or other possessions? How can it affect the friendship?**
- **Do you trust your friends with your favorite personal items? Why or why not?**

***

The dance on Saturday night was a lot of fun, and Siobhan thought Gretchen looked great in the borrowed pink top. Gretchen was going camping with her family for a few days after that, so Siobhan didn't expect to hear from Gretchen or get the top back right away. But when Gretchen returned to school in the middle of the next week, Siobhan was waiting at her locker.

"Hey, could you bring my pink top to school tomorrow?" Siobhan asked.

"Sure," Gretchen said, flipping through a notebook. But the next day came and went—and still no pink top.

Siobhan was growing frustrated—it wasn't like Gretchen to not return something as soon as she could. That pink top was Siobhan's favorite, and Gretchen knew it. That night, she sent a series of texts to Gretchen, getting angrier as each went unanswered.

"Hey, can you bring my top tomorrow, please?"

"I'd like to wear it this weekend, so maybe write yourself a note."

"Why aren't you answering my texts?"

"Seriously, Gretchen, I just want the top back."

"Fine then. Steal my clothes. Whatever."

"Gonna stalk your locker for the rest of the week. Never lending you anything again. Night."

***

The next morning, Gretchen was waiting at Siobhan's locker. For the first time since they met in eighth grade, Siobhan couldn't read the expression on her best friend's face.

"Check your bag," Gretchen said quietly, nodding toward Siobhan's favorite tote that she carried everywhere.

TALK ABOUT IT

- **What do you think of Siobhan's reactions to Gretchen, from the first conversation at her locker to the final text?**
- **Have you ever had a friend not return something that was important to you? How did you handle it?**

Not knowing what else to do, Siobhan opened her bag and dug through the contents to find the pink top balled up and wedged inside.

Then she remembered. After the dance on Saturday, Gretchen had met Siobhan in the girls' room and returned the top, pulling on a T-shirt she'd brought along. "So I don't forget after the camping trip," Gretchen had said before she and Siobhan hugged goodbye.

Siobhan opened her bag and dug through the contents to find the pink top balled up and wedged inside.

"When we got back from camping, I found out my grandma's really sick," Gretchen

Even if Gretchen hadn't gotten that awful news, she knew her mean texts hadn't been necessary.

said, looking down at her shoes. "She's probably not going to make it much longer. That's why I forgot yesterday when you asked for the top back. And then we were at the hospital last night, and I left my phone at home." Gretchen's eyes brimmed with tears. "Then I saw your texts."

Siobhan's heart sank. Even if Gretchen hadn't gotten that awful news, she knew her mean texts hadn't been necessary.

"But don't worry," Gretchen said, turning around. She looked over her shoulder at Siobhan. "I'll never ask you to lend me anything again."

Siobhan felt like such a jerk. Why had she been so quick to get angry at her best friend? And she hadn't even bothered to ask whether anything was wrong. Siobhan knew Gretchen was close to her grandmother, and she knew her friend must

TALK ABOUT IT

- **What do you think Siobhan should do now, and why?**
- **Do you think Gretchen and Siobhan will make up? Why or why not?**

be feeling awful right now. There was no excuse for how she had acted. Siobhan needed to make things right.

***

The next day, Siobhan was waiting at Gretchen's locker when the final bell rang.

"Can we talk?" she asked. Gretchen nodded. "You can go first, if you want," Siobhan said.

"It really hurt when you flew off the handle like that," Gretchen said. "I could have told you about my grandma, I know, but I was really distracted and dealing with the fact that we're probably going to lose her soon." She looked down, and Siobhan could tell Gretchen was trying not to cry.

"I'm so sorry," Siobhan said. "About your grandma, of course, and for being so petty about the top. I shouldn't have acted that way. I hope you know I'm here for you."

"Thanks," said Gretchen. She held out her arms, and Siobhan hugged her tight. "I've really missed you."

TALK ABOUT IT

- **What were the steps Siobhan took to make the situation right with Gretchen?**
- **What could you do to resolve a conflict with a friend?**
- **What would you have done if you were Siobhan? If you were Gretchen?**

ASK THE EXPERT

Even though you and your friends might have drama, it's important not to immediately give up on them. Some conflicts may be deal breakers if they involve serious matters, but if you discard friends over minor arguments, you may find yourself with no friends at all. Remember that conflicts between friends can and will happen, and they often arise out of misunderstandings or miscommunication.

Close friendships involve intimacy and commitment, so every mistake might feel like the end of the world. This may explain why Siobhan was confused and frustrated when Gretchen, who was normally good about returning borrowed items, supposedly failed to return Siobhan's favorite top.

When Siobhan realized her mistake and overreaction, she knew she needed to apologize. She let Gretchen speak her feelings first and sincerely apologized, showing Gretchen that she was there for her during that difficult time. With an apology and a little time, the girls can repair their friendship and move on stronger than ever.

GET HEALTHY

- Remember that it's normal for friends to disagree and have miscommunications. What's important is how friends handle their disagreements.
- In-person conversations can be difficult but are ultimately an effective way to work out a misunderstanding or disagreement.
- Use simple and clear language, and don't make accusations.
- Practice the conversation in front of your mirror or with someone else if you're nervous about talking to your friend.
- Don't end friendships over minor mistakes or misunderstandings.

THE LAST WORD FROM LAUREN

Even best friends argue. If you really want a relationship with someone, you have to learn how to communicate with one another. Avoiding conflict can lead to resentment and anger down the road. In other words, if you don't handle the small drama, it can lead to much bigger drama later. Siobhan let a misunderstanding lead to drama, but she realized her mistake, gave Gretchen some space, and apologized, giving them both the opportunity to repair their friendship and move on. The steps to resolution aren't too hard—you just have to know them and practice!

CHAPTER FOUR

FRIENDS VS. BULLIES

Rumor mills and gossip girls are everywhere, but what happens when teasing escalates into bullying? Making fun of someone for things such as weight, race, and sexuality is never OK—that should be obvious. But how do you deal with a friend who has become a bully? Do you speak up and risk your status with your pal, in your friend group, and at school? Or do you let it slide and hope things work themselves out? Going to an adult can feel like betraying your friends, but how do you know when you no longer have a choice?

Many schools and organizations now teach anti-bullying workshops. Even so, real-life bullying situations aren't always easy to navigate. Gossip and rumors can be tools bullies use with destructive results. Jae-Suh thought Charlotte was a good friend, but when Charlotte started picking on a classmate going through a major life change, Jae-Suh was uncertain how to handle it.

JAE-SUH'S STORY

"Hey, Megan, I love your skirt," Charlotte cooed at her classmate, who smiled and thanked her. After Megan sat down, though, Charlotte turned to her best friend, Jae-Suh, and said, "That is the ugliest skirt I've ever seen. I think Megan's been shopping at Goodwill again."

Jae-Suh wasn't sure what to do. Tall, imposing, and ranked first in the class academically, Charlotte had been her best friend since they met in academic decathlon last year. As nice as she was to Jae-Suh, who tended to be quiet and shy, Charlotte liked to talk about people behind their backs, and lately her remarks were getting meaner.

Charlotte liked to talk about people behind their backs, and lately her remarks were getting meaner.

"Uh . . ." Jae-Suh said, but Charlotte had already moved on to another victim.

"Brian's looking especially gay today," Charlotte whispered as another classmate passed them. "Why are his pants so tight?" Just then, Brian looked their way, and Charlotte called, "Hello," waving at him with a sweet smile on her face.

Jae-Suh felt awful. Megan's family didn't have much money—most people knew that. She couldn't help it if she couldn't afford nice clothes. And why should Charlotte care if Brian wanted to wear tight pants? Jae-Suh was straight and smart, and her parents were doctors, so she figured she was safe from Charlotte's wrath—but she still felt strange seeing her friend act

TALK ABOUT IT

- Do you think Charlotte's gossiping could be considered bullying? Why or why not?
- Have you ever seen a friend's personality start to change for the worse? How did you react?
- What should Jae-Suh do about Charlotte's remarks?

nice to these people's faces and then insult them behind their backs.

***

The next day, Jae-Suh brought up Charlotte's nasty words to a mutual friend. She knew that it was technically gossip, but she didn't know where else to turn. Jae-Suh's parents frequently worked late, and she wasn't sure they'd understand anyway.

> Jae-Suh brought up Charlotte's nasty words to a mutual friend. . . . She didn't know where else to turn.

To Jae-Suh's disappointment, the friend just shrugged. "She's just stressed about her grades, and that's her way of venting," the friend whispered before the bell rang at the end of biology class. Jae-Suh thought about talking to Charlotte herself—or even sticking up for the kids Charlotte talked about—but she worried that then Charlotte would start telling other people nasty things about her instead.

Then Theo, a sophomore classmate who was just as quiet and shy as Jae-Suh had been when she was younger, publicly came out as transgender. Theo was assigned male at birth but identified as female. Theo decided to keep her name for the time being but was starting to use *she/her* pronouns instead of *he/him*. Jae-Suh had never met a transgender person before, but she understood that Theo was just being who she was.

For the most part, kids were supportive—but Charlotte, who had never paid attention to Theo before, zeroed in on the transgender girl. Charlotte started loudly commenting on Theo's clothes whenever she walked by Theo in the hallway. Once, she said she wondered whether Theo shopped in the "she-male"

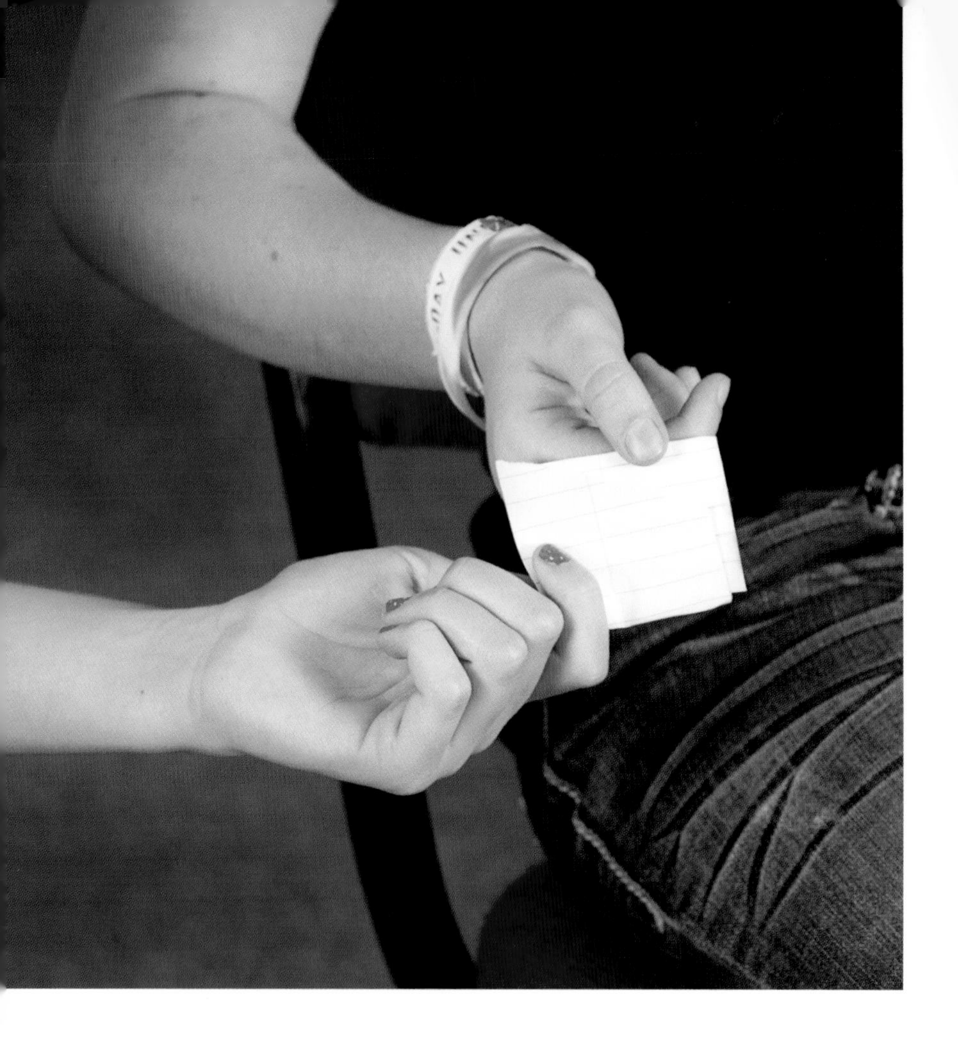

TALK ABOUT IT

- What would you do if you were singled out because of your race, class, sexuality, or other factors?
- Have you ever stood by while someone you knew engaged in bullying behavior? How did it make you feel?
- Why do you think people make fun of others?

section of clothing stores. Jae-Suh was walking next to Charlotte and two of their friends when Charlotte made this comment. Jae-Suh cringed, as did another friend, but neither girl said anything.

***

"Check this out," Charlotte whispered to Jae-Suh the next day. She showed Jae-Suh a handwritten note that said, "Are you a boy or a girl? Check one," before folding it up. Jae-Suh's blood ran cold. She'd just read about a transgender teen the next state over who had died by suicide because of remarks like Charlotte's. But still, Jae-Suh watched hopelessly as Charlotte stuck the note into Theo's locker.

Jae-Suh was torn. She had hoped Charlotte's bullying would go away on its own, but it only seemed to be getting worse. And now Jae-Suh was worried about Theo. Being the only out transgender kid in school couldn't be easy, and naturally, mean remarks and notes making fun of Theo's gender wouldn't help. Jae-Suh wondered whether Charlotte's other friends felt the same way but, like Jae-Suh, were afraid to speak up.

She had hoped Charlotte's bullying would go away on its own, but it only seemed to be getting worse.

Jae-Suh remembered how Charlotte had loaned her lunch money countless times when Jae-Suh forgot her own, helped her with studying for academic decathlon, and treated her to movies and concerts, never expecting Jae-Suh to pay. She'd been a good friend to Jae-Suh

for almost two years. It was tough to admit, but Jae-Suh had to face the fact that Charlotte was changing. Even with their history, Jae-Suh couldn't stand by and just watch Charlotte bully others.

TALK ABOUT IT

- **What do you think will happen to Jae-Suh now? To Theo?**
- **Do you think Jae-Suh did the right thing? Should she have spoken up sooner? Why do you think that?**
- **Have you ever confronted a bully? What was the result? Looking back, is there anything you would have done differently?**

***

"Ugh, did you see Theo wearing a *skirt* today?" Charlotte said loudly the next morning as she and Jae-Suh stood by her locker. "Who does he think he is, a real girl?" She laughed.

Jae-Suh took a deep breath. "You know what, Charlotte? Theo *is* a real girl. And she is *she*, not *he*."

Charlotte looked at Jae-Suh, taken aback. "Uh . . ." she said, a smirk growing on her pretty face.

Jae-Suh cut her off. "I've listened to you make fun of people who didn't deserve it, and I'm done saying nothing. It's not OK. I can't be around you when you act like this. If this doesn't stop, I think I'm done with you." She slung her backpack over her shoulder and walked away.

The bell rang as Jae-Suh headed to her first class. She knew Charlotte might start bullying her next, but she didn't regret standing up for Theo.

ASK THE EXPERT

We all get stressed out, and it's good to have friends as a sounding board. But venting is not an excuse for bullying. Venting is talking about a bad experience to try to understand and process it. Charlotte might very well be stressed about school, but she could have expressed her anxiety to Jae-Suh or her other friends instead of tearing other people down.

At first, Charlotte was gossiping—talking about someone on purpose to make them look bad. When she started making comments about Theo so Theo could hear, this behavior became bullying. Often, gossip can descend into bullying behaviors like ganging up on someone, deliberately excluding them, and—as Charlotte did to Theo—targeting them. It's important to speak up for others, just as Jae-Suh did. When Jae-Suh and her friends just watched, they were bystanders. But when Jae-Suh took action, she became an ally. An ally is anyone who acts when she sees bullying happening. Those actions can include stepping in to stop the bully, changing the topic, or speaking to the bully. Jae-Suh's friendship with Charlotte may be over, but her stronger sense of self is just beginning.

GET HEALTHY

- Recognize when a friend's words and actions are destructive to you and others.
- If you hear a friend gossip or see her bully someone else, you can speak up. Express to your friend that it's immature and that it upsets you to see her put others down.
- If you're not comfortable talking to your friend directly, there are other ways to help. Even changing the subject or saying something funny can work well. You can also reach out to the victim and show your support.
- If you suspect someone will be in danger because of the bullying, get an adult involved.

THE LAST WORD FROM LAUREN

When I was in junior high, I was the target of bullies. Unfortunately, the bullying descended into physical assault, and my parents as well as the school principal had to get involved. Things died down by the time I reached high school, but I never forgot the friends who stuck by me, walking with me down hallways so no one would bother me and even speaking up on my behalf. As I made more friends, I did my best to pay it forward by reaching out to the victims around me and making sure they knew they weren't alone.

No one wants to be the target of a bully. If you were bullied, would you want someone to speak up for you? I'm willing to bet the answer is yes. So next time a "friend" gossips about others, keep that in mind. Doing the right thing can be difficult, but I bet you'll sleep a lot better at night.

Social Media
Google
Instagram
Twitter
YouTube
LinkedIn
WhatsApp
Pinterest
LINE
LINE
Facebook

CHAPTER FIVE

TAKING DRAMA ONLINE

How much time do you spend online? Most likely a lot. Technology is such an important part of life now. We shop, read books, and watch our favorite TV shows from the comfort of our phones—not to mention doing research for school and taking fun quizzes about what kind of cheese we'd be. And of course, a big part of how we use technology is to talk to others through texting, email, and social media.

There's a lot to love about communication by technology. You can text your mom about dinner, your best friend about a crush, and your dance teacher about running late to class—all in less than a minute! You can also find friends with mutual interests from all over the world and sometimes connect with them in

real life. But social media and the internet have a dark side too. For Caroline, what started as an innocent argument with a friend quickly spiraled into online bullying. She learned the hard way what harm social media can do—such as ruining someone's reputation just by typing and hitting Send.

CAROLINE'S STORY

Caroline and Margaret hardly ever fought. They'd been friends since sixth grade when they met at gymnastics camp. They stayed close even after Caroline made the elite competition team and Margaret decided gymnastics was no longer for her. Now that they were 16, Margaret concentrated more on her social life while Caroline kept an intense schedule of gymnastics training and advanced classes. But they had a standing sleepover the second Saturday of every month, sat together at lunch, and texted constantly. Caroline figured that if gymnastics couldn't keep them apart, nothing could. She was wrong.

Social media and the internet have a dark side too.

It started late one night after Caroline came back from training and finished her homework. She got a text from Margaret.

"Hey, can we sit with Vanessa and her friends tomorrow?"

Caroline hesitated. Vanessa and that crowd were into partying, and Caroline knew they looked down on her for studying and training so hard. Besides, Caroline liked her alone time with Margaret. She texted Margaret back, "I don't know."

"Really? I ask to mix it up once, and you won't do it? So nice, Care."

Now Caroline was surprised. She and Margaret hung out in different groups, sure, but neither of them were ever this hostile.

"Are you OK?" she replied. "You seem off."

No answer. Caroline figured she could be honest.

"I just don't want to hear Vanessa talk about how drunk she got last weekend. I get enough of that sitting next to her in

French class. It gets real old, real fast. How many times can a person brag about throwing up without sounding like a moron?"

Now Caroline, tired from homework and gymnastics and really not in the mood to debate with Margaret, was getting heated up, and her thumbs flew over the keyboard. "Honestly, I don't know why you hang out with those burnouts. You're better than they are."

A text bubble popped up right away.

"Have fun with your musclehead buddies instead of getting a life. You can eat alone tomorrow."

Caroline's heart sank.

***

The next morning at school, Caroline noticed people eyeing her as she made her way to her locker. Some rolled their eyes and looked away, but others looked like they felt sorry for her. What was going on? Caroline tapped her locker neighbor Nora on the shoulder.

"Um, is there something I should know?" she quietly asked Nora.

TALK ABOUT IT

- **Have you and a friend ever disagreed about another person's choices, such as drinking and partying? How did you handle it?**
- **Have you ever gotten a text from a friend that was angrier than usual? How did you respond?**
- **How do you think Caroline should have responded?**

Nora looked around and then leaned in. “I think you need to see this. I’m so sorry,” she said, showing Caroline her phone, eyes wide with sympathy.

The words jumped up in all caps like they were screaming: CAROLINE O'BRIEN IS A MEAN GIRL. It was a private social media group, but it had a lot of members already. In it, Margaret had posted screenshots of their text conversation last night when Caroline had insulted Vanessa. Margaret had conveniently edited out her own part of the conversation.

Margaret had conveniently omitted her own texts, in which she said things that were just as bad or worse.

And that wasn't the only post. There were a *lot* of screenshots of private text conversations between Margaret and Caroline, in which Caroline was less than nice about several classmates. Again, Margaret had conveniently omitted her own texts, in which she said things that were just as bad or worse. The comments were from kids Caroline didn't even know, and they were terrible, saying what a horrible person Caroline was. More than one person even suggested she kill herself.

"I feel sick," Caroline murmured before running to the bathroom. She didn't really, but she couldn't face pre-calc. What had Margaret done?

***

Caroline stayed in the bathroom for most of first period. This was bad. Everybody gossiped. So what? Nothing she had said had been particularly terrible—but seeing weeks of texts clumped together, she realized she had been nastier than she had meant to be.

TALK ABOUT IT

- **Why do you think Margaret started a secret group to trash Caroline?**
- **How might you feel if someone shared screenshots of texts that were meant to be private?**
- **How should Caroline handle this situation?**

But still, why had Margaret done this? It was just a simple argument over where to sit at lunch. Caroline knew Margaret was having trouble at school, and maybe there were other things going on Caroline didn't know about, but did Margaret have to be this extreme?

"Can you send me screenshots of the group?" Caroline texted Nora. Soon, Caroline's phone started lighting up as Nora did what she asked. Caroline knew what she should do next. She had to tell an adult.

***

As soon as the bell rang for the beginning of second period—when the hallways were quiet and safe—Caroline knocked on the door of her guidance counselor, Ms. Fey. Luckily, the counselor didn't have an appointment and was free to talk. Pulling out her phone and showing Ms. Fey the screenshots Nora had texted her, Caroline told her counselor everything. She felt like a tattletale, but she really didn't know where else to turn.

"What should I do?" Caroline asked, trying to keep her voice steady. Wasn't talking about your problems supposed to make you feel better? Instead, she had to keep from sobbing all over Ms. Fey's desk.

Ms. Fey took off her glasses and pinched the bridge of her nose. Her silence was not what Caroline wanted to hear. "They did *not* cover this in grad school," Ms. Fey finally said. She looked tired. "I hate to say this, Caroline," she continued, "but I really can't do anything about a fight over a text that got out of hand. Unless Margaret got physical with you, I'm not sure what you expect me to do about it." She put her glasses back on and pushed them up her nose. "You'll see this more and more as you get older. Some girls are just mean."

TALK ABOUT IT

- **Should Caroline go to another adult about this? Do you think she'll get the same reaction? Why or why not?**
- **If Caroline decides to handle the situation on her own, what do you think she should do?**
- **Should Caroline just ignore this drama with Margaret? Why or why not?**
- **What would you do if you were the target of cyberbullying?**

As the bell rang and Caroline stepped out of Ms. Fey's office, she felt stuck. She felt like the answer Ms. Fey gave her was a cop-out. She was certain that Ms. Fey should have done more to help. Should she tell her parents? But if an adult whose job it was to help her wouldn't do anything, what could her mom and dad do?

Then Caroline realized what she needed to do. She took a deep breath and pulled out her phone. She texted Nora again.

"I think I need to talk to Margaret, but I don't want to do it alone. Can you come with me?"

She held her breath until Nora's reply popped up on her screen. "For sure. Just tell me where and when."

***

When the final bell rang and Margaret got to her locker, Caroline and Nora were waiting.

Margaret rolled her eyes when she saw them. "What do you want?"

Caroline held up her phone, displaying a screenshot of the secret group. "To talk about this." When Margaret looked away, Caroline counted to ten in her head, forcing herself to stay calm. Before going on, she looked at Nora, who nodded encouragingly. "Margaret, I'm sorry I insulted your friends. But I wish you would have told me it bothered you instead of starting a whole hate campaign against me."

Now Margaret looked up at Caroline. "Maybe don't be so judgmental." She turned back to her locker, but Caroline and Nora didn't budge, so Margaret turned around again. "What?"

TALK ABOUT IT

- **Do you think Caroline did the right thing by talking to Margaret with a friend by her side? Why or why not?**
- **What are some other things Caroline could have done if she didn't feel comfortable speaking with Margaret?**

Caroline raised her eyebrows. “Maybe take it down? Now?”

Margaret let out a long sigh. “Fine.” She pulled out her phone and made a big show of deleting the group. “Happy?”

“Yes,” Caroline and Nora said.

Margaret glared at Caroline. “Have fun sitting alone at lunch.”

Caroline’s heart sank, but Nora linked her arm through Caroline’s. “Who says she’ll be alone?” Caroline smiled at her friend, and she and Nora made their way out of the school.

ASK THE EXPERT

It's not unusual for drama to unfold on social media—whether it escalates into cyberbullying or not. There's not necessarily more drama now than there was before social media, but there's much more of a risk of drama going public. To make matters worse, studies have shown that intense use of digital technology can actually interfere with personal relationships.

This doesn't mean you have to delete all your accounts and swear off text messaging forever. Digital communication can be a great thing if used wisely. And many times (as in Margaret's case), a bully can also be dealing with her own drama. Still, that doesn't make it OK for the bully to take it out on you. If you're having a conflict with a friend, try not to take it online. And if the bullying escalates, don't be afraid to go to an adult. It is the school personnel's job to stop all kinds of bullying. Some adults don't know what to do either, so they might downplay the situation. Even if the first one you approach writes off the bully's behavior as "girls being mean," try another adult until you find one who understands and will help.

GET **HEALTHY**

- Do your best to act the same online as you would face-to-face.
- You don't have to like everybody you meet, but don't send snarky texts or post mean statements. What's written can be easily misconstrued, even if you meant it to be funny.
- If you are cyberbullied, don't engage by commenting or retaliate by starting your own secret group. That can feel good in the moment but escalate very quickly.
- If the cyberbullying gets extreme, write down everything (or take screenshots) and go to a parent or trusted adult.

THE LAST WORD FROM **LAUREN**

When I was in high school, cyberbullying wasn't really an issue. Social media wasn't nearly as widespread as it is now. In this day and age, though, odds are good that any big drama will be talked about digitally—whether it's in private texts that can easily be screenshotted and shared, in a message thread, or even in a secret social media page that eventually becomes not-so-secret.

I'm no cyberbully, but even as an adult, I have to remind myself not to take personal drama online. It's so tempting sometimes, especially since social media is primarily how my friends and I stay in touch. But I know from experience that one misplaced word or unkind text may lead to hurt feelings, anger, and in the end, much more drama. Thankfully, I've never been the target of cyberbullying, but I've witnessed through other friends how destructive it can be. If you become a victim of this, don't be afraid to ask a friend or adult to have your back.

CHAPTER SIX

RESOLUTION

"It's OK to be angry." How many times have you heard that sentence? If you're like me, probably a lot. But hearing a statement is one thing, and living it is another. As girls, we're often expected to let things slide or to not make too big a deal about a mean remark or action. We may be told it's OK to be angry, but meanwhile, we're also receiving some very different messages.

But here's the thing about anger: not only is it a normal emotion but it also can have a positive effect when it's respectfully expressed. It's definitely possible to vent your feelings and ask for change without being hurtful. Educator and author Rosalind Wiseman has a great strategy for this, which she calls SEAL.

SEAL stands for Stop and Strategize, Explain, Affirm, and Lock. In the first step, stop and strategize, ask yourself whom the conflict is with and what it is about, and then determine when and where you'll talk to that person. When you talk, explain how the conflict makes you feel and what you would like to happen. Then, affirm what rights you and the other person have and what your role in the conflict is. Finally, lock in what you want the relationship to be. Lacey used the SEAL strategy to deal with her anger in a healthy way.

LACEY'S STORY

"You have a great voice."

Lacey looked up to see whom her best friend, Morgan, was talking to. It was Alexandra, the new girl in their soprano section in choir.

"Thanks," Alexandra said coolly, adjusting her sheet music. Lacey had to admit that Morgan was right. During just one rehearsal, Alexandra had demonstrated her perfect pitch and stunning voice. Lacey glanced at her best friend. Clearly, Morgan had stars in her eyes over the new girl.

Lacey remembered when Morgan had said "You have a great voice" to her too. When she met Morgan, who also sang soprano and had taken voice lessons since fifth grade, the two clicked immediately. They rehearsed together after school, saved one another seats in class and on buses for out-of-town music festivals, and they even went in together to pay for semiprivate voice lessons. Thanks to Morgan, Lacey learned to love singing even more.

Lacey glanced at her best friend. Clearly, Morgan had stars in her eyes over the new girl.

"What are you looking at?" Alexandra asked Lacey, her voice tinged with judgment.

Lacey blushed. "Nothing, just spaced out for a second."

"Hmm." Alexandra looked Lacey, in her T-shirt and jeans, up and down before turning away with indifference. Alexandra was wearing a short skirt and high-heeled boots. Lacey wondered whether Alexandra didn't approve of her style.

"She's so cool," Morgan breathed when the bell rang and Alexandra strutted away.

Lacey wasn't sure she agreed, but she said nothing.

"Let's see if she wants to hang out this weekend," Morgan said. Lacey didn't want to be mean, so she agreed.

***

As the semester went on, Lacey noticed little ways Morgan was changing. She no longer wanted to stay after school and rehearse with Lacey, giving excuses after class or just ignoring Lacey's texts altogether. One Saturday, Lacey asked Morgan to hang out.

"Sorry, I'm helping my grandma today," Morgan said. Later, though, Lacey was scrolling through her social media and saw photos of Morgan and Alexandra at the mall, big smiles on their faces. Morgan's grandmother was nowhere in sight.

When the first music competition came along, Lacey boarded the bus and went to sit by Morgan. "This seat's for Alexandra," Morgan said as Alexandra slid into the seat from behind Lacey.

TALK ABOUT IT

- **Did you ever have a new friend join you and your best friend? What happened? How did it work out?**
- **Do you think Lacey should give Alexandra a chance, knowing Morgan likes her so much? Why or why not?**

Alexandra was smirking. Her face burning, Lacey quickly went to find another seat. Through the whole trip she could hear Alexandra and Morgan whispering and laughing, sometimes

TALK ABOUT IT

- How do you think Lacey feels?
- How would you feel if a friend left you behind for someone new? How would you deal with it?
- What do you think Lacey should do now?

looking her way before whispering some more.

Lacey decided to try reconnecting with Morgan again. One day after choir—they had stopped sitting together at this point—Lacey approached Morgan, who was glued to

Alexandra's side. "Hey Morgan," Lacey said. "I was thinking of doing another semiprivate lesson. You in?"

Morgan folded her arms and shifted her weight on her new high-heeled boots. "I don't think so. Alexandra says I'm more on her level," Morgan said.

Alexandra chimed in. "Rehearsing with you is holding her back."

Lacey really wanted to yell at Morgan at that point. Instead, she quickly turned around and headed for the hallway so Morgan wouldn't see the tears in her eyes.

***

The next day, after sleeping on it, Lacey sent a text to Morgan: "Is everything OK?"

She was surprised when Morgan texted back a few hours later, "Why?" It was a very different response from Morgan's usual long and involved texts. Still, Lacey was hopeful they could work things out. Morgan didn't respond to any more of Lacey's texts

Lacey really wanted to yell at Morgan. . . . Instead, she quickly turned around . . . so Morgan wouldn't see the tears in her eyes.

that day. So Lacey thought carefully about what she would say when she saw Morgan next.

***

"Hey," was all Morgan said when they met at her locker the next day. She looked annoyed.

Lacey thought carefully about what she would say when she saw Morgan next.

Lacey noticed Morgan was dressed in a short skirt, thigh-high socks, and a cropped sweater. It was nothing like Morgan's usual jeans-and-a-T-shirt look and *exactly* like Alexandra's look. Instead of making a snarky remark about it, though, Lacey took a deep breath and tried to remember SEAL, the conflict-resolution method she had learned about in psychology class.

She'd already completed the first step, coming up with a plan to talk to Morgan. She had to remember to choose her words carefully.

"I feel like you've been blowing me off lately," Lacey said slowly, trying to keep her voice neutral so Morgan wouldn't get defensive. "You're not answering texts or sitting by me in choir, and that hurts my feelings. I know you really like Alexandra, and maybe I haven't given her much of a chance, but I'd love it if we could start being friends again." She had been looking down at her hands, but now she looked Morgan straight in the eye. "I don't want to lose you."

Morgan rolled her eyes. "Sorry I'm not a good enough *friend* to you." The bell rang, and she strutted away without another word.

Lacey felt stung, and during choir she made sure to avoid both Alexandra and Morgan. Morgan didn't look Lacey's way even once. As the last bell rang, Lacey's phone buzzed. She looked down to see a text from Jasmine, another friend from choir who had graduated the year before. Now she was at college across the country.

"Ugh, I am so homesick. I feel like a baby, but I really miss singing with y'all."

As she headed to her locker, Lacey hit *call* and put the phone to her ear. She decided to make Jasmine a care package with homemade cookies when she got home. When Jasmine answered, Lacey smiled. "Hey, fellow soprano, what's up?"

TALK ABOUT IT

- **How do you think Lacey handled the situation with Morgan? Is there anything you would have done differently?**
- **Why do you think Morgan reacted the way she did?**
- **Do you think Lacey and Morgan can be friends again? What about Lacey and Alexandra?**
- **Have you ever confronted a friend? What did you do, and how did it go? Looking back, would you do anything differently?**

ASK THE EXPERT

Anger can be positive. You don't have to yell or throw around insults to get your point across—that's likely not going to get the results you want. However, there are different ways to express anger toward a friend.

Lacey used a version of the SEAL method. The first step is to stop and strategize. Instead of going off on Morgan and Alexandra after choir class, Lacey walked away and approached Morgan later to talk.

Second, explain what happened that you didn't like and what you would like to happen. Again, Lacey did this perfectly. Instead of accusing Morgan or using absolutes like *always* and *never*, she explained that her feelings were hurt when Morgan had stopped answering her texts and sitting by her and that she wanted to be friends again.

The third step is to affirm anything you did to contribute to the conflict but also realize that you and the other person are worthy of respect. Lacey admitted that maybe she hadn't given Alexandra a fair chance, but she stood her ground instead of letting Morgan push her around.

Finally, you lock the friendship in or out or take a break. In this case, Lacey didn't get an apology. But instead of forcing the issue or chasing after Morgan, Lacey decided to take a break from her friendship with Morgan and focus on another friend: Jasmine. The SEAL strategy can help you get through a confrontation in the most effective way possible while acknowledging that your own feelings are legitimate.

GET HEALTHY

- When you're angry at a friend, remember that your feelings are important and being angry is not "overreacting."
- If you decide to talk to your friend directly, take time to gather your thoughts and plan your words.
- Use Rosalind Wiseman's SEAL strategy: stop and strategize, explain, affirm, and lock.
- Recognize that you won't always get the outcome you want—resolution might not mean that you get an apology.

THE LAST WORD FROM LAUREN

When I was writing this book, I came across the phrase *bitter versus better.* At first, this saying may sound simplistic, even silly. However, this can be a great mantra for dealing with anger that stems from friend drama. Bitter versus better is a method of handling hurt feelings—choosing to stay angry or be mistrustful (bitter) or learning from the experience and moving on (better).

Anger is just fine, and confrontation can be cathartic. Once you've used the SEAL method, let go of your anger and turn it into something positive. Do a good deed. Help out at home, or reach out to another friend who might need a little extra love. Instead of feeling bitter, feel better!

CHAPTER SEVEN

DRAMA QUEEN

We all deal with drama—but what happens when the drama starts with *you*? This can be hard to admit. Even when we're causing problems ourselves, it's much easier to point fingers at someone else. Sooner or later you may be the one causing drama, and it's important to know how to deal with that.

Looking back at my teen years, I definitely caused some drama by saying things I shouldn't have while knowing those comments would hurt others or by deliberately excluding people from my friend group. At some point, you may look around and wonder, *Why do others seem afraid of me? What did I do to deserve this?* Popular Karyn had to take a hard look inward at her past drama queen behavior.

KARYN'S STORY

"Are you *kidding*?" Karyn said to her friends Catie and Audrey after school. "Debra had no right to blow me off like that!"

"Like what?" Catie asked.

"She totally ignored me when I said hi to her in the bathroom just now," Karyn said, feeling her blood pressure start to spike.

Audrey rolled her eyes. "So? Maybe she was having a bad day. Why do you always make such a big deal out of stuff like this? Not everything's about you, Karyn."

Karyn and her group were the most popular clique in school. Recently, Karyn learned she was front-runner for homecoming queen, a big deal at their school, and she was currently scouring local stores and online shops for the perfect dress. She didn't have a date, but she and her friends were looking forward to tearing up the dance floor.

Karyn considered herself a nice person most of the time. She just didn't like when girls deliberately ignored her when she said hello—especially girls like Debra who weren't as popular. Karyn felt that she deserved to be acknowledged.

TALK ABOUT IT

- **What do you think of Karyn's reaction to Debra?**
- **Audrey tells Karyn, "Not everything is about you." Was that fair to say? Why or why not?**

"Whatever," Karyn said to Audrey. Just then, Debra walked by them in the courtyard. "Did you see that dress she's wearing today? She looks like she's pregnant."

Karyn made sure to say that last sentence extra loudly. She saw Debra's face fall as the girl quickly walked away. *That'll teach her to ignore me,* Karyn thought.

Karyn and her group were the most popular clique in school.

***

Two weeks later, the homecoming queen voting results were tabulated. Karyn was surprised to learn she was only runner-up. Sophie, another senior girl, was the winner. "*Sophie*?" Karyn huffed at lunch, pushing her salad around on her plate. She looked at her friends. "She's not even that pretty!"

To Karyn's shock, Audrey threw her hands in the air, exasperated. "She's *nice*. People aren't afraid of her like they are of you." Catie nodded in agreement.

"I'm so sick of this, Karyn. . . . You're really self-centered."

"What?" Karyn was genuinely shocked. "People are *afraid* of me? How did I not know this?"

Catie picked up her tray. "I'm so sick of this, Karyn. You take

everything personally. You're really self-centered. And you know what? I didn't vote for you either." She left the lunch table.

"Can you believe her?" Karyn said to Audrey. She couldn't get over her own shock. Audrey had been silent during Catie's outburst. Now she looked up from her rice bowl.

TALK ABOUT IT

- **How would you feel if your classmates were afraid of you?**
- **Have you ever been afraid of or nervous around a popular girl? Why or why not?**
- **Why do you think others are afraid of Karyn?**

"You really do overreact to everything. We've both thought that for a long time."

"The Debra thing?" Karyn asked. Audrey nodded. "OK, that was once. I'm allowed to be upset if someone's mean to me."

"She wasn't mean," Audrey said. "She might not have even heard you! And it wasn't just once. Last year, Rebecca got a better grade than you on the geometry midterm, and you cried really loudly right in front of her to make her feel bad. Even last month, you called Raye a slut when John asked her to the homecoming dance instead of you."

Karyn had heard enough. "Whatever," she said, picking up her tray and trying to ignore the feelings of guilt that were creeping up inside. "I think I'm done here." *I am not giving a ride to Audrey and Catie today,* Karyn thought.

***

After school that day, Karyn cranked up her favorite radio station and cruised home. As the angry girl–rock pulsed in her ears, she thought about what her friends had said at the lunch table. Karyn always thought she just told it like it was and was proud of her lack of filter.

In fact, Karyn always thought her brutal honesty was what made her popular. In a way, she supposed, that was still true. But rather than make people like her, she thought, what if that quality made others afraid of her?

Truthfully, Karyn thought Sophie was a goody-goody. She was always organizing food drives for the local homeless shelter and volunteering for after-school peer tutoring, while Karyn preferred to binge-watch Netflix with her friends and hunt online for the best deals on secondhand designer clothes. Sophie's style was bland—nowhere near as funky and unique as her own, Karyn thought with a smile.

TALK ABOUT IT

- **Has another friend ever called you out? How did you react?**
- **Why do you think Audrey and Catie waited until now to remind Karyn of the drama she's caused in the past?**

Was Audrey right, though? Did Karyn make too much out of the little things and lash out as a result? Karyn then remembered seventh and eighth grade. She was an outcast back then, uncomfortable with her own body as it changed and unsure of her personal style. Because Karyn wasn't very confident, she had

been a target for some of the mean girls who had since gone to a different high school. Karyn realized that four years later, she'd become the mean girl.

Pulling into her driveway, Karyn turned off the ignition and rested her head against the steering wheel. She was beginning to realize that maybe she got what she deserved.

She then texted Audrey, who she now realized had been honest with her about what a drama queen she was. That couldn't have been easy to do. "Hey, you were right—I do kinda make everything about me," she wrote. "Thanks for calling me out. Are we still good?"

TALK ABOUT IT

- **What should Karyn do about her realization that classmates might be afraid of her?**
- **How is Karyn's type of popularity different from Sophie's?**
- **Do you know peers like Karyn and Sophie? How do you and others see them?**

ASK THE EXPERT

Often, people may convince themselves that their negative behavior is a result of someone else's actions. It's always easier to blame someone else. For example, Karyn thought that her remarks about other girls in high school were justified because she herself was teased in junior high. Once she got the power in high school, Karyn felt she had a right to turn the drama around on others.

Outsiders and targets—used to being the subjects of drama—can easily turn around and become queen bees themselves for fear of being outsiders and targets again. It always feels better to be on top, which is why Karyn's equally popular friends didn't say anything earlier. Additionally, drama (especially gossip) can feel like a bonding experience between friends. Audrey and Catie joined in on the teasing or at the very least stood by and didn't defend the other girls. Now that Karyn has had this realization, maybe she will act differently toward those who made their feelings known by electing Sophie, a genuinely likable person.

GET **HEALTHY**

- Avoid spreading rumors, name-calling, and talking behind others' backs. These are behaviors that can quickly lead to drama.
- Remember that even if you were once the target of a drama queen, that doesn't make it OK for you to turn around and make drama for others.
- Find ways to bond with your friends that don't involve gossip. Try to keep your words and actions positive, especially involving those outside your group.
- If you want to make it up to those you teased or gossiped about, a simple and sincere apology is the way to go.

THE LAST WORD FROM **LAUREN**

Popularity can look very different depending on the person. In Sophie's case, she was popular because she was genuinely nice and worked actively to help others. Karyn's popularity, however, was a result of fear—which was a result of the drama she caused. I definitely knew people like both Sophie and Karyn when I was in high school, and I bet you do too. Whom would *you* vote onto the homecoming court?

It can be easy to fall into the gossip trap with your friends. After all, you're not going to like everybody, and some people are just asking for it, right? Wrong. Do your best to avoid becoming a drama queen. And if appropriate, apologize to those for whom you've caused drama, and don't repeat the mistakes you've made. It's never too late to start fresh!

CHAPTER EIGHT

SHARING A CRUSH

Crushes happen all the time. They can be a lot of fun—the heart-pounding excitement when you get a text from your crush, the spike of adrenaline when a crush follows you on social media—and they can also cause a lot of heartbreak. Sometimes your crush feels the same way about you. Other times, he or she might not return your feelings or even know you're alive.

Crushes can be dramatic in and of themselves, but when you and a friend share a crush, how do you deal with the seemingly inevitable drama? Sure, it can be fun to giggle over a crush's cute sense of style or plan to "accidentally" bump into that person. But more likely than not, the crush will choose one of you—or neither of you. When that happens, how can your friendship continue?

When best friends Jenny and Bette both started crushing on Tim, the new guy in school, they were initially able to bond over him. Soon, however, things got messy.

BETTE'S STORY

"Have you seen the new guy, Tim?" Jenny asked Bette after school the first day of junior year.

Bette shut her locker and shouldered her backpack. "I totally have! He's in my honors English class." She and Jenny had gone to school with most of their classmates since kindergarten, so anyone new was automatically interesting. And Tim, with his broad shoulders and thoughtful brown-eyed gaze, was very interesting.

Jenny motioned for Bette to come closer and whispered excitedly, "He's in my French class, and he sat by me!"

Bette was happy for her friend. Jenny was shy around boys. She definitely liked them—she'd told Bette—but she didn't know what to say or do when they paid attention to her. It was fun to see Jenny blush and giggle over a guy.

Just then, Tim walked by and grinned at both of them before tossing his soccer cleats over his shoulder and making his way down the hall.

Jenny sighed. "So cute."

"I know!" Bette said. The girls squealed together and then burst out laughing.

***

For the next few weeks, Jenny and Bette talked of almost nothing except Tim. They texted back and forth about his talent

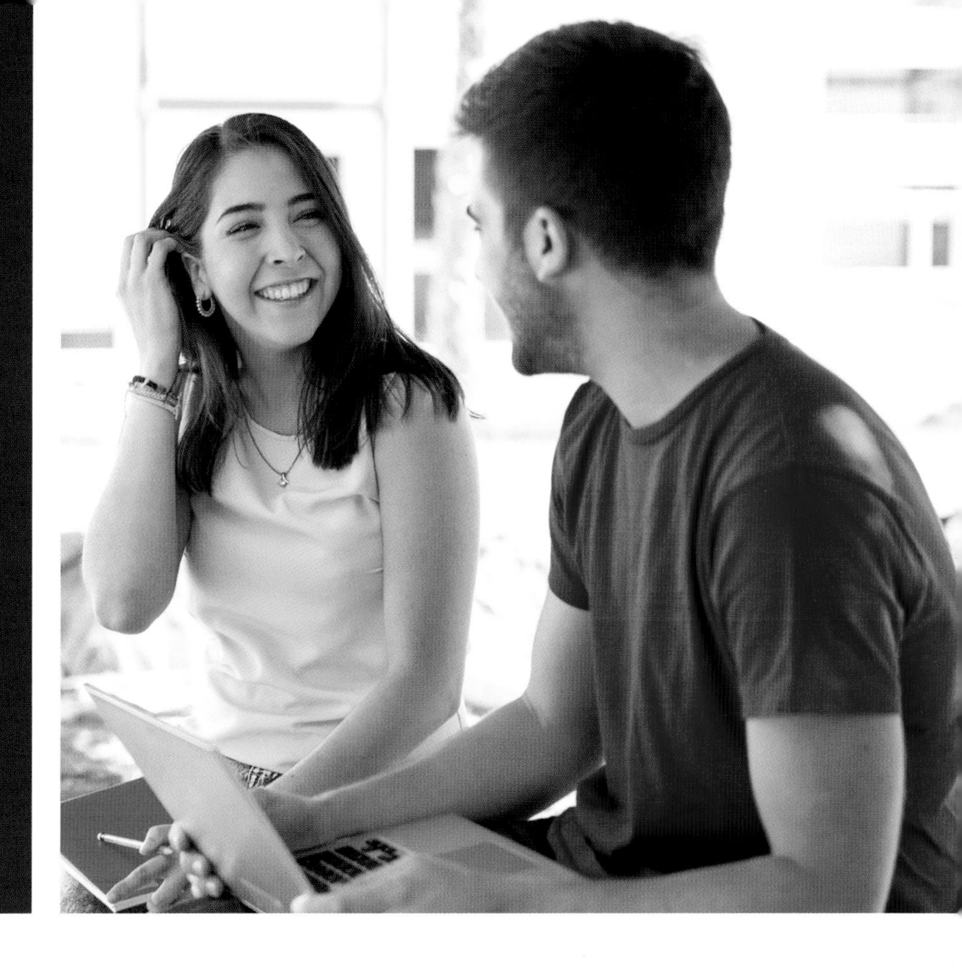

on the soccer field and his thoughtful analysis of *Hamlet*. When Tim invited Jenny to be part of a study group for French, she rushed to Bette's locker after class and gave Bette a play-by-play.

At first, sharing their crush was fun for Bette. She and Jenny were bonding as Jenny came out of her shell. But one day when Tim passed them both in the hallway, Bette noticed how he smiled right at Jenny. It was like Bette wasn't even there.

TALK ABOUT IT

- **How do you normally react to new classmates?**
- **Do you or your friends feel awkward around potential crushes? Why or why not?**
- **Have you and a friend ever experienced a mutual crush?**

Bette wasn't mad exactly—Jenny hadn't done anything wrong—but Bette started to realize this mutual crush wasn't going to end well for either of them.

The next day at lunch, Jenny started her usual gushing about Tim. Bette knew she was supposed to join in—after all, that had been their routine for weeks. But she couldn't stop thinking about Tim smiling at Jenny. Bette had tossed and turned the night

before, thinking about what would happen next—he'd ask Jenny out, they'd become the school's *It* couple, and Bette would be left in the dust with her unrequited feelings for Tim.

Bette rolled her eyes at her friend. "Can you talk about something other than a *guy*? You're a smart girl, Jen. It's beneath you."

Jenny's smile faded, and she looked down at her fries. "Well, that's new. I thought you'd want to hear about study group. Tim looked really adorable today."

Bette started to realize this mutual crush wasn't going to end well for either of them.

Bette shook her head, realizing she'd hurt her best friend's feelings. "I'm sorry. I just . . . it was fun to like Tim, but I worry it's going to come between us. I mean, what if he chooses one of us?" Now Jenny looked worried, so Bette kept going. "You're my best friend, and I don't want to lose you over a guy." She took a deep breath. "Do you think we can stop liking him?"

Jenny didn't answer at first, and Bette held her breath. "I, uh, I really like Tim," Jenny said. "And you know it's been hard for me to talk to guys sometimes, but he's . . . easy to talk to." Then Jenny nodded. "But you're right. You're the most important person to me, and I don't want some dumb guy to ruin that."

She reached across the table and took Bette's hand. "No more Tim talk. I promise."

Bette squeezed Jenny's hand. "You're the best."

"I know," Jenny joked. She half smiled and looked away.

Should I have asked her to give up on a guy she really likes? Bette wondered, but she tamped down her guilt. *If Jenny liked Tim, she could find another guy too. This is the right thing for both of us. I know it.*

"You're the most important person to me, and I don't want some dumb guy to ruin that."

***

For the next week or so, everything seemed fine. Bette noticed Jenny was quieter than usual, but they were getting close to midterms, so she figured her friend was just stressed. But on a Friday morning, Bette got out of English class to find Jenny waiting by her locker, looking worried.

TALK ABOUT IT

- **What do you think of Bette's solution?**
- **How would you have handled this situation if you were Bette? What if you were Jenny?**
- **How do you think Jenny is feeling right now?**

“I have to talk to you,” Jenny said, lowering her voice to a whisper.

A dozen bad scenarios ran through Bette’s head: *Was Jenny sick? Had someone teased her sensitive best friend?* Bette would kill whoever it was if that were the case.

“Of course,” she whispered back, leaning in. “What’s wrong?”

Jenny looked down at her sneakers. “Tim asked me to a movie tomorrow night.”

Bette’s heart dropped down to her own shoes. “Oh,” was all she could think to say. And she could tell by the way Jenny was biting her lip that this wasn’t the whole story.

"You want to go, don't you?" Bette asked.

Jenny nodded. "I *know* we said we wouldn't like him anymore, and I was *fine* with that, I swear," she said, green eyes wide. "You're way more important to me than any guy, and I didn't want to get into a fight. But . . ." She trailed off.

Bette had known Jenny since kindergarten, and she knew that look on her friend's face. Jenny was scared, but serious. "You really like him, don't you?" Bette took a deep breath, knowing what she had to say next, even though it was hard. "You should go."

Jenny's entire face lit up. "Really? You mean it?"

Bette nodded, pasting a smile on her face. "Really. Have fun."

Jenny gave her a tight hug. "Thank you so much!" She pulled out her phone. "I'm gonna text him right now!"

Bette had seen this coming, of course, since the day she saw Tim smiling at Jenny and not her. In a way, she didn't blame him. Jenny was smart, funny, and pretty, and she deserved a guy who saw all of her good qualities and appreciated them. Still, before now, Bette had still held out a little bit of hope that Tim would choose *her*.

As Jenny happily texted away, Bette watched, knowing she'd done the right thing but wishing it didn't hurt so much.

TALK ABOUT IT

- **Why do you think Bette told Jenny to go out with Tim? What would you have done?**
- **How do you think this will affect Jenny and Bette's friendship?**
- **Do you think Bette will regret her decision? Why or why not?**

ASK THE EXPERT

Having crushes is natural, but not every crush will turn into a relationship. In fact, most of them won't. More often than not, crushes are based on physical attraction and infatuation and occur when you don't know much about the other person. Take Bette and Jenny for example. They both developed a crush on Tim during the first day of school, when he was new and no one knew him very well.

Often, crushes fade when you get to know your crush better as a person. Less often, they develop into something more substantial. And when you and your friend share a crush, there's a risk of hurt feelings from one or both of you. There's also a risk the crush might "choose" one of you, and the other might feel left out.

Though Bette initially lashed out at Jenny, she eventually was open with her friend that the mutual crush was making her uncomfortable. Bette was also gracious when Tim asked Jenny out, even though she still had feelings for him. It was hard for her to do, but Bette communicated clearly with Jenny, which bodes well for the future of their friendship.

GET **HEALTHY**

- If having a mutual crush with your friend is fun, enjoy it!
- Know that most crushes fade. It's not worth ending a friendship over something that will likely be temporary.
- If you're uncomfortable sharing a crush, talk about it with your friend.
- Don't hold in your feelings and then take them out on your friend.
- Remember that your crush is a human being, not a prize to be won.

THE LAST WORD FROM **LAUREN**

My high school was very small, and most of us had known each other since kindergarten. Any new person was automatically exciting and different, which led to a lot of shared crushes like Bette and Jenny's. More than one argument went down in the hallway when the fun stopped and feelings clashed. Looking back, I wish my friends and I had known that having honest conversations with one another may be tough in the moment but is ultimately healthier in the long run.

Don't let new romantic feelings get in the way of an already-existing friendship. Having crushes can be a lot of fun and lead to new connections, whether they're romantic or platonic. But the friendships you already have shouldn't go by the wayside because you're into the same person. Shared crushes happen, and they aren't the end of the world—just be open with your feelings and communicate with your friend! No matter what happens with the crush, you'll be setting the groundwork for a long-lasting relationship with your pal.

A SECOND LOOK

Drama exists on a spectrum. You can define *drama* as everything from a tiff with a friend over where to sit at lunch to a major blowout involving personal texts shared online for the whole school to see. And there are many ways to deal with drama, depending on the situation. You can say, "Hey, that's not OK." You can end the friendship altogether, or you can keep your distance until graduation day.

Knowing the various options you have—everything from speaking up to finding a new group of pals—is not only important in high school but also with the drama you'll experience as an adult. Because we're human, we'll clash from time to time, and it's important to know how to handle these clashes. By learning to deal with drama now, you're practicing for the relationships you'll have in adulthood while also improving the friendships you have now.

Even when you know how to deal with drama, it can be easy to get caught up in disagreements with friends, bad behavior from frenemies, and potentially destructive gossip. Sometimes, your friends (and the drama around them) will feel like your whole world. Remember to keep everything in perspective. Even in the smallest of environments, there are possibilities for resolution, help, and new beginnings. You may be able to handle one conflict completely on your own. Other times you may need to call on an adult you trust—and there's no shame in either approach.

I hope this book has given you a lot to think about and explore. Because drama is inevitable, it's important to be aware of the options you have. An open mind and perspective are essential tools. Once you have both, your relationship with drama will be a whole lot less murky.

XOXO,
LAUREN

PAY IT FORWARD

Dealing with drama is all about growth. Discovering what makes you feel your best is a journey that changes throughout your life. Now that you know what to focus on, you can pay it forward to a friend too. Remember the Get Healthy tips throughout this book, and then take these steps to get healthy and get going.

1. **As you grow older, know that friendships change and evolve. Be open to developing new interests and forming new friendships. Don't be afraid to go outside your comfort zone!**

2. **You can stay in your friend group even if someone in it is bothering you. Just keep your distance from that person and concentrate on your other friends.**

3. **If there is conflict between you and a friend, try to work it out face-to-face rather than over text.**

4. **Try not to take problems with friends online, whether that's sending negative messages or starting a chat or group on social media.**

5. **Know that both experiencing conflict and venting can be normal and healthy but bullying and gossiping are not.**

6. **Don't hold in negative emotions you have toward a friend. Communicate as simply and as clearly as you can.**

7. **If you are being bullied in person or online, tell a parent, teacher, or other trusted adult. Write down dates, times, and incidents of the bullying. Or if the bullying is online, take screenshots.**

8. **If you've caused drama with a person or a group and want to make up for it, try a simple and clear apology—and remember that the person may or may not accept it.**

9. **Prioritize kindness, authenticity, and humility when working through drama.**

10. **Use Rosalind Wiseman's SEAL strategy for conflict resolution: stop and strategize, explain, affirm, and lock.**

GLOSSARY

academic decathlon

An academic competition consisting of a speech, a performed quiz, an interview, an essay, and seven tests to prove knowledge across different subjects.

ally

A person or group who gives help to another person or group.

bystander

A person who is present at an event or incident but doesn't participate or intervene.

cathartic

Relieving of one's emotions or tension.

crush

A brief but intense romantic feeling for someone else.

cyberbullying

Using the internet to bully or harass, including by sending intimidating messages, posting unwanted photos and videos, or creating false profiles.

escalate

To increase in intensity.

gossip
Conversation about other people used to make them look bad, typically including personal information or rumors.

midterm
An exam given at the middle of an academic term.

outcast
A person who is denied belonging to a certain group.

platonic
Regarding a close relationship that is friendly, not romantic.

screenshot
An image that captures what is on a phone or computer display.

venting
Talking or communicating, usually with intensity, about a bad experience in order to express feelings and understand what happened.

ADDITIONAL

RESOURCES

SELECTED BIBLIOGRAPHY

Damour, Lisa. *Untangled: Guiding Teenage Girls through the Seven Transitions into Adulthood.* Ballantine Books, 2016.

Sales, Nancy Jo. *American Girls: Social Media and the Secret Lives of Teenagers.* Penguin Random House, 2017.

Wiseman, Rosalind. *Queen Bees and Wannabes.* 3rd ed., Harmony, 2016.

FURTHER READINGS

Carnegie, Donna Dale. *How to Win Friends and Influence People for Teen Girls.* Simon & Schuster, 2020.

Huddleston, Emma. *Healthy Friendships.* Abdo, 2021.

Skeen, Michelle, and Kelly Skeen. *Just As You Are.* Instant Help, 2018.

ONLINE RESOURCES

To learn more about dealing with drama, please visit **abdobooklinks.com** or scan this QR code. These links are routinely monitored and updated to provide the most current information available.

MORE INFORMATION

For more information on this subject, contact or visit the following organizations:

Girls, Inc.

120 Wall St., Eighteenth Floor
New York, NY 10005
girlsinc.org
212-509-2000

This national organization focuses on long-term mentoring relationships and research-based programming to help girls grow up healthy, independent, and educated.

I Am B.E.A.U.T.I.F.U.L.

4850 Golden Pkwy., Suite B230
Buford, GA 30518
iambeautiful.org
404-545-9051

This educational nonprofit helps women and girls of all ages to build self-esteem and leadership skills. Programs support success in every aspect of life.

The Megan Meier Foundation

515 Jefferson St., Suite A
Saint Charles, MO 63301
meganmeierfoundation.org
636-757-3501

Founded in 2007, this nonprofit has resources on dealing with bullying and cyberbullying. It also provides leadership training to teens, parents, and educators.

INDEX

ABOUT THE AUTHOR

LAUREN EMILY WHALEN

Lauren Emily Whalen lives in Chicago with her cat, Versace. She's written for publications like *BUST* and *SELF* magazines and is the author of two young adult novels. Lauren was a theater major at Loyola University Chicago and is very familiar with drama of all kinds. She hopes this book will help you learn to deal with your own drama!